Based on the episode "The Bat in the Belfry"
written by Duane Capizzi

Adapted by Jack Oliver,
additional text for this edition by
Simon Mugford
Illustrated by Rick Burchett
Colour by Lee Loughridge
Designed by John Daly

Batman created by Bob Kane

Published by Ladybird Books Ltd
A Penguin Company
Penguin Books Ltd, 80 Strand, London WC2R 0RL, England
Penguin (Group) Australia, 250 Camberwell Road, Camberwell, Victoria 3124, Australia.
Penguin Group (NZ) 67 Apollo Drive, Mairangi Bay, Auckland, New Zealand.

GOING BATTY © 2005 DC Comics
Batman and all related characters and elements are trademarks of DC Comics © 2005.

Published by Ladybird Books 2006
1 3 5 7 9 10 8 6 4 2

ISBN-10 1-84646-184-7
ISBN-13 978-1-84646-184-2

Printed in Italy

Bruce Wayne was reluctantly attending a Gotham Gators basketball game when he received a message on his Batwave saying that there had been a gas explosion outside Arkham Asylum.

It was with some relief that the publicity-shy billionaire made his excuses to his companions and left.

At Arkham Asylum, an orderly named
Slack was working the night shift.
Making a checklist, he saw that all of
the inmates were in their cells, but
one cell that he thought was empty
appeared to be occupied.

"I wasn't told about any new
arrivals," he said to himself.

Slack unlocked the door and came
face to face with his surprise guest.

"I was feeling a bit screwloose, so I
checked myself in!" the stranger said.

"Who are you?" Slack asked.

"Let me introduce myself," cackled
the Joker, as he showed Slack his card
and sprayed him with a mysterious gas.

The Joker's gas explosion had caused mayhem, releasing prisoners from the east wing of the asylum and blocking the access road. Batman arrived to find the police attending a chaotic scene.

Knowing that there was only one way in and not wishing to attract attention to himself, Batman used his grappling hook to silently swing above the streets and into Arkham Asylum.

"It's time to get to the bottom of this mess," he said to himself.

Batman made his way to the cells and found the poor orderly suffering from the effect of Joker's laughing gas. He was slumped on the floor, not moving and with his mouth stretched into a terrible grimace. Batman quickly realized what had happened and threw a Batarang before the Joker could spray him with the poison too.

"You've ruined my new hideout," Joker said to Batman, "and my old place was so regal!"

The Joker managed to escape Batman's grasp and cackled, "Happy Days are coming to this town!"

Batman picked up Slack and took him to the Batcave.

Back at the Batcave, Batman's trusted butler, Alfred, laid Slack down and after a brief examination said, "Besides being a prisoner in his own body and having an awful smile, this chap's as fit as a fiddle."

Batman knew that he needed to find the Joker and collect a sample of his terrible laughing gas. Without an antidote soon, the madman was going to be able to give the whole of Gotham a frozen smile!

Batman remembered that Joker said he'd been hiding somewhere "regal" before he came to the asylum. The old Monarch Playing Card Company factory appeared to fit that description and sure enough, Batman found the Joker there, preparing his evil plan.

"Have you heard the one about the clown and the bat?" said Joker.

But Batman was in no mood for jokes. "Where are you hiding the gas?" he asked.

Joker just laughed. "Don't worry, Bat, I'll soon fix your sense of humour!"

Batman realized that the Joker had a balloon filled with laughing gas and that he was somehow going to release it over Gotham! He got into the Batmobile and sped through the city streets as Joker drifted through the sky above.

The balloon was heading towards a warrior statue with a sharp sword. Joker laughed crazily from the basket as he guided his poisonous cargo towards the sword's tip.

Batman sprang into action, using his grappling hook to swing up to the balloon.

"Stop this thing now, Joker!" he shouted.

"What with? Air brakes?" laughed Joker, waving a huge pair of scissors.

As the balloon drifted dangerously close to the statue's sword, Batman tried to pull himself closer to the madman in the basket. At the same time, he sent out a signal that summoned his Batboat.

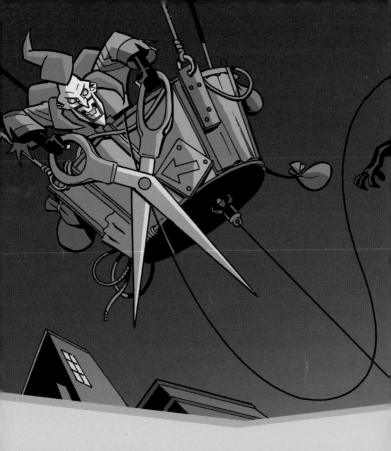

"It was nice to see you, Bat, but I'm afraid I'm going to have to cut your little visit short!" shouted Joker, as he tried to cut Batman's line with his scissors.

The balloon was swinging wildly, but
Batman used all of his strength to cling
on. Then he pushed a button on his
belt and the Batboat immediately fired
a huge Batarang which locked into the
bottom of Joker's balloon.

"Hold tight, Joker" said Batman, "and get ready for a crash landing!"

The Batboat began to speed towards Gotham Harbour, pulling Joker's gas balloon with it and away from the sharp point of the warrior statue's sword.

The sudden movement caught Joker off guard, and Batman quickly swung himself into the basket and kicked Joker hard in the chest with both feet. Batman and Joker fought as the Batboat kept on pulling the balloon.

The Batboat eventually dragged the balloon right into the water and the poison gas seeped out, taking effect on some unfortunate fish. Batman wrestled with Joker, eventually overcoming him.

Batman managed to collect a small sample of the gas. He took the sample back to the Batcave and Alfred was soon able to make some antidote to treat poor Slack.

Slack was soon back at work at
Arkham Asylum and was more than
happy to lock up its newest inmate.

"This is definitely not what I had in
mind," shouted Joker. "It would appear
that I've gone a little bit BATTY!"